Dear Parents and Educators,

Welcome to Penguin Young Readers! As parents and educators, you know that each child develops at his or her own pace—in terms of speech, critical thinking, and, of course, reading. Penguin Young Readers recognizes this fact. As a result, each Penguin Young Readers book is assigned a traditional easy-to-read level (1–4) as well as a Guided Reading Level (A–P). Both of these systems will help you choose the right book for your child. Please refer to the back of each book for specific leveling information. Penguin Young Readers features esteemed authors and illustrators, stories about favorite characters, fascinating nonfiction, and more!

Peter Rabbit™
I Am Peter

LEVEL **2**

GUIDED
READING
LEVEL **F**

This book is perfect for a **Progressing Reader** who:
- can figure out unknown words by using picture and context clues;
- can recognize beginning, middle, and ending sounds;
- can make and confirm predictions about what will happen in the text; and
- can distinguish between fiction and nonfiction.

Here are some **activities** you can do during and after reading this book:
- Word Repetition: Reread the story and count how many times you read the following words: *angry, help, hop, plan, want*. On a separate sheet of paper, work with the child to write a new sentence for each word.
- Make Predictions: In this story, Peter, Benjamin, and Lily get into trouble. First, they run into Mr. McGregor in his garden. Then they see Mr. Tod in the woods. What do you think will happen? How will they escape?

Remember, sharing the love of reading with a child is the best gift you can give!

—Bonnie Bader, EdM
    Penguin Young Readers program

*Penguin Young Readers are leveled by independent reviewers applying the standards developed by Irene Fountas and Gay Su Pinnell in *Matching Books to Readers: Using Leveled Books in Guided Reading*, Heinemann, 1999.

PENGUIN YOUNG READERS
Published by the Penguin Group
Penguin Group (USA) LLC, 375 Hudson Street, New York, New York 10014, USA

USA | Canada | UK | Ireland | Australia | New Zealand | India | South Africa | China

penguin.com
A Penguin Random House Company

Published by Penguin Young Readers, an imprint of Penguin Group (USA) LLC,
345 Hudson Street, New York, New York 10014. Manufactured in China.

Library of Congress Cataloging-in-Publication Data is available.

ISBN 978-0-14-135006-6 (pbk)   10 9 8 7 6 5 4 3 2 1
ISBN 978-0-14-135004-2 (hc)   10 9 8 7 6 5 4 3 2 1

I Am Peter

Penguin Young Readers
An Imprint of Penguin Group (USA) LLC

I am Peter.

Peter Rabbit.

I live with my mom

and my three sisters.

Sometimes my mom wants me to stay home.

She wants me to help clean.

She wants me to help cook.

She wants me to help my sisters.

But I want to go outside.

I want to go outside with my
friends Benjamin and Lily.
We have a lot of fun together.

But sometimes we get into trouble.

We sneak into the garden.

There are carrots!

Radishes!

Apples!

Oh no, someone is coming!

We better hop to it!

We lost him.

I think we are safe.

I have a plan.

We will go back to the garden.

Oh no.

That was not a good idea.

We better hop to it!

We lost her.

I think we are safe.

I have a plan.

We have carrots.

And we have lots of radishes.

Now we can eat.

Oh no.

He wants to eat the carrots.

He wants to eat the radishes.

He wants to eat us!

We better hop to it!

We lost him.

I think we are safe.

I have a plan.

We will go to the lake.

Oh no.

We were too loud.

He is angry.

We better hop to it.

We lost him.

I think we are safe.

I have a plan.

We will go to the woods.

Oh no.

We woke him up.

He is angry.

We better hop to it!

We are safe at last in our treehouse.